Galjoen

Maasbanker

Pilchard

ARMIEN'S FISHING TRIP

TRIP CATHERINE STOCK

Yellowtail

Kabeljou

Barbel

hite Stumpnose

MORROW JUNIOR BOOKS

NEW YORK

Special thanks to Armien and Amelia Abrahams, Jaap Bosschieter, George Curtis, Revel and Suzanne Fox, Vincent Cloete, Alan Kirkaldy, and Meredith Charpentier for their contributions and encouragement.

———————————————————

Printed in Hong Kong by South China Printing Company (1988) Ltd.
1 2 3 4 5 6 7 8 9 10
Library of Congress Cataloging-in-Publication Data
Stock, Catherine.
Armien's fishing trip
/ Catherine Stock.
p.   cm.
Summary: While visiting his aunt and uncle in the little South
African village of Kalk Bay, Armien stows away in his uncle's
fishing boat and becomes an unexpected hero.
ISBN 0-688-08395-1. —ISBN 0-688-08396-X (lib. bdg.)
[1. Fishing—Fiction.   2. South Africa—Fiction.]
I. Title.
PZ7.S8635Ar   1990
[E]—dc19   89-3266   CIP   AC

The little village of Kalk Bay is tucked under the western mountains of False Bay on the southern tip of Africa. Two hundred years ago the area was settled by Filipino fishermen, European sailors, and freed slaves from Malaya and Java. This diversity of fishing skills and seafaring experience made the Kalk Bay crews the finest on the coast.

Many families were forced to leave when the village was declared "white" in 1967 under the South African government's Group Areas Act. There was tremendous local opposition, and eventually the government relented, but not before much damage had been done. Of the original community of two hundred "coloured" families in 1967, only about seventy-four remain today.

This book is dedicated to the fishermen of Kalk Bay and to all the people who worked to preserve the community and its way of life.

Armien is a Muslim name pronounced AH-min.

It was Saturday morning.

Pweeeeeeeee. The Kalk Bay train whistled on its way down the coast.

Armien breathed in the fresh salty air and waved to the people on the beach. He wished that he still lived here instead of on the hot and sandy Cape Flats.

Aunt Amelia was at the station to meet him.

"Here's my big boy coming to spend the weekend with his old auntie!" she said, hugging him warmly. "And now tell me about your mother and sisters and how you like your new school."

"They're all fine," Armien answered. His eyes searched the harbor. "Where is Uncle Faried?"

"The *Rosie* went out at four this morning," said Aunt Amelia. "The men will be back at midday."

"Armien, Armien!" His old schoolfriends Boeta, Talip, and Fred shouted up from the harbor beach. "Come fishing with us."

"Off you go, then," said Aunt Amelia. "You'll tell me your news later. I'll bring down some nice homemade samoosas for your lunch."

"Mmmm, my favorite." Armien squeezed his aunt and ran off to join his friends.

The boys made their way to the steps behind the breakwater. Talip handed Armien a line, and they baited their hooks with pilchards.

"Yesterday I caught the biggest fish you ever saw," bragged Boeta.

"It was nothing as big as mine last week," Fred insisted.

"Hey, Armien, what kind of fish you got on the Flats? *Goldfish?*" The boys laughed at their joke.

Armien scowled. "You laugh now, Boeta. Tomorrow I'm going out on my uncle's boat and I'll catch a fish bigger than all three of you."

"You're going out on the *Rosie?*" The boys stared at Armien.

He nodded and swallowed hard. "Sure. I'm going out with all the men to do some real fishing."

"Man, my pa won't ever take me out." Boeta was impressed. "You lucky fish."

At midday, the *Rosie* chugged into the harbor, followed by shrieking gulls. Two harbor seals raced out to greet the boat.

"You two are the greediest seals in the ocean," Uncle Faried shouted, tossing them each a maasbanker. "Hello, Armien."

Sam, the oldest fisherman in Kalk Bay, threw a rope up for Armien to loop over a bollard. "Good to see you again, young friend." His wrinkled brown face creased into a toothy grin.

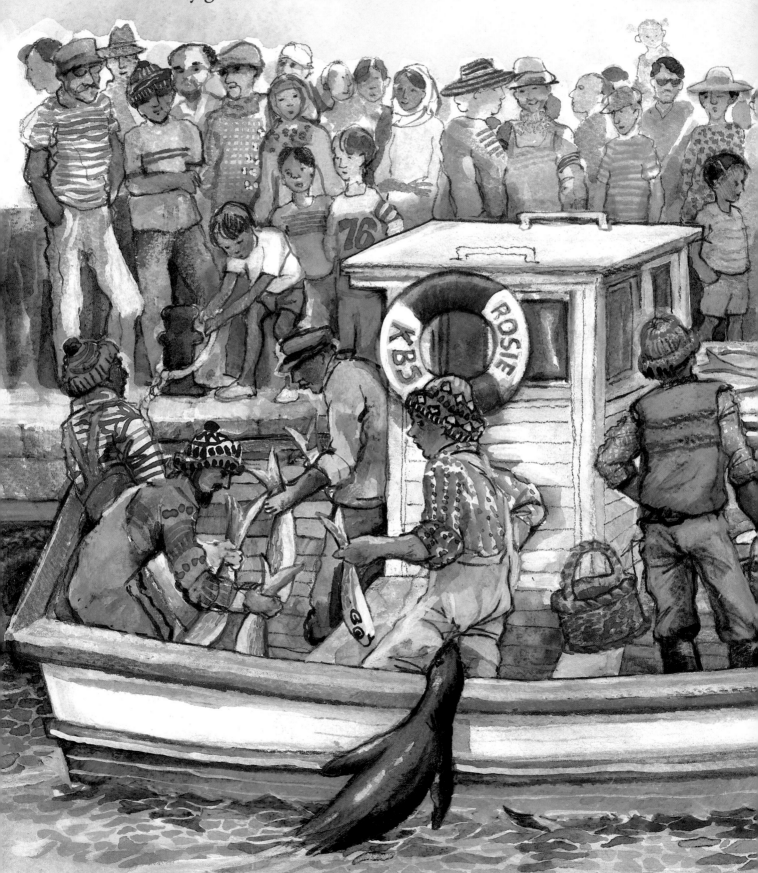

Suddenly the jetty was alive with people shouting and haggling over the fish.

"Five rands for this nice kabeljou!"

"Yellowtail—fifteen bob, fifteen bob, fifteen bob!"

"Stumpnose, white stumpnose!"

Armien carried a customer's yellowtail over to the shed where his aunt cleaned fish.

"Hello, dear," she said. "Did you find your uncle?"

"Yes." Armien paused. He scuffed his tennis shoe along the cement step. "Aunt Amelia, do you think that Uncle Faried would take me out on the boat tomorrow?"

"You on the *Rosie*? Don't be a rascal. A boat is no place for little boys." She took a packet from her apron pocket and pressed it into his hands. "Here are your samoosas, still nice and hot from the stove. Off with you, now. Look at all these fish I must clean."

Armien bit into a samoosa and trudged back to the jetty to find his uncle. The samoosa was crisp and stuffed with fragrant curried lamb and vegetables. But Armien wasn't hungry anymore.

Uncle Faried was washing down the *Rosie*. Armien jumped into the boat to help him.

"You know, Armien, your grandfather and his father and his father all fished out of Kalk Bay."

"I'm going to be a fisherman, too," said Armien.

"It's a hard life, Armien, and a dangerous one. But if salt water runs through your veins, there's nothing else like it."

"Uncle Faried…"

"What is it, my boy?"

"Nothing," Armien muttered. What was the use? His uncle wouldn't take him out on the *Rosie*. He would have to prove to them all that he was old enough for the sea.

Armien woke up early the next morning. It was dark and still. Stars shone through his open window.

Thump…bump, bump. Uncle Faried was getting ready to go fishing.

Armien slid quietly from his bed and dressed quickly. *Brrrrr.* It was cold.

He pulled on a heavy jersey, grabbed his waterproof jacket, and climbed out through the window.

Armien's rubber boots thumped down the cobblestone alley and past the cafe to the harbor. Men stood about in pools of lamplight, warming their hands around mugs of steaming coffee.

He was the first person to get to the *Rosie,* except for old Sam, who slept on the boat. Armien watched Sam unlock the cabin and shuffle around the deck.

Like a cat's shadow Armien crept onto the boat and slipped down the open hatch. Once the men discovered him out at sea, it would be too late to turn back.

Soon the other men started to arrive.

"I don't know, Piet." It was his uncle's voice. "The harbor may be quiet enough, but it's probably howling out in the bay."

"Ja, but those kabeljou are really biting out by Kaptein's Klip, Skipper. We don't want to miss this run."

"All right," Armien heard his uncle reluctantly agree. "But it's going to be a rough trip."

The diesel engine started up, and the boat chugged out the harbor entrance and into the open sea.

Uncle Faried was right. The farther out they went, the rougher it got. The *Rosie* lurched up and down the steep troughs of water and rolled from side to side. Armien clung to his bunk. He felt terrible. Now he knew why the fishermen chuckled about the summer tourists who pleaded to be taken out on the boats. "Not a pair of sea legs in the lot," Sam would say, shaking his head.

Armien groaned and closed his eyes.

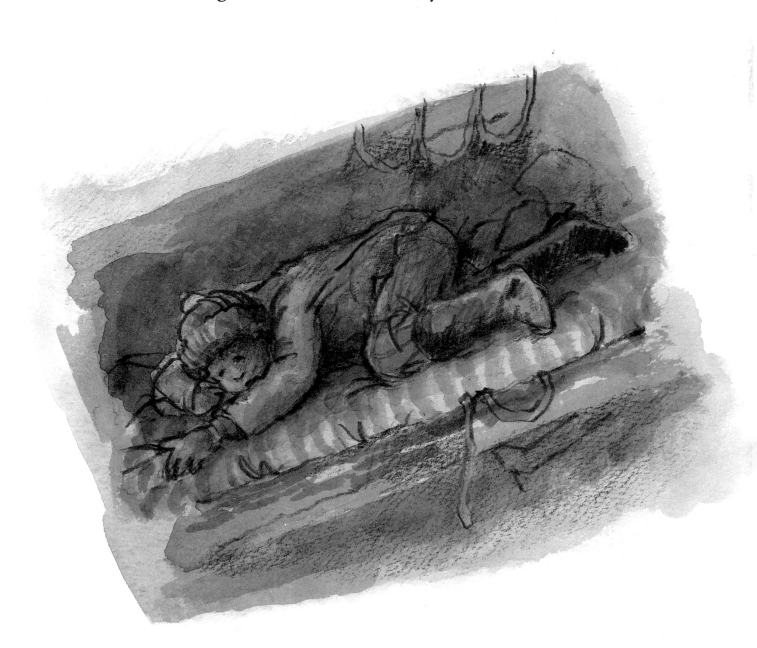

Finally the engine spluttered to a stop. Armien heard the men clamber to the front of the boat and throw the heavy anchor overboard.

At last it was safe to go on deck. Armien scrambled up the ladder and breathed deeply.

Old Sam was at the back of the boat, carefully slicing bait. He grunted as his sharp fishing knife dropped from his knotty old fingers and slid across the deck. Slowly he rose to pick it up.

Just at that moment a huge wave crashed against the *Rosie*'s starboard side. It threw Armien off his feet, and he tumbled in a wet heap against the side of the boat.

"*Owwwww,*" he groaned, rubbing a bruised elbow. He wiped the hair from his eyes and struggled to his feet.

He was alone on the deck. Where was Sam? He had been right there a second ago!

"Sam! Sam!" Armien screamed.

"Help...." A faint voice rose over the side of the boat and was snatched by the wind.

Armien wrenched a life ring from the side of the cabin and threw it to Sam.

"Armien!" Uncle Faried grabbed him by the shoulders. "What are you doing here?"

"Uncle Faried—the wave—Sam—Sam—" Armien cried wildly. "Quickly!"

The men ran to the side of the boat and peered into the stormy sea.

A little red light bobbed in the dark.

"There he is!" shouted Armien.

Uncle Faried ripped off his heavy jacket and boots and dived out toward the light.

He reached Sam, who was clinging to the ring with the last of his strength. Dragging Sam through the crashing waves, Uncle Faried fought his way back to the *Rosie*.

First the men pulled Sam to safety, and then they helped Uncle Faried onto the boat.

Piet found blankets in the hold and wrapped them around the two drenched men while Armien poured out mugs of hot coffee.

"You saved my life, Faried," Sam said at last. "It was a brave thing to do, coming into the water like that."

Uncle Faried hesitated a moment, then put his arm around Armien. "Sam," he said quietly, "you owe your life as much to Armien here as to me."

A red and lavender dawn crept slowly across the
horizon, and the wind drifted away in the paling sky.
Uncle Faried started up the engine, the men heaved in
the anchor, and they headed home.

When the *Rosie* got back to the harbor, Aunt Amelia was there with half the people of Kalk Bay, including Boeta, Talip, and Fred.

"Armien, I've been worried sick about you!" Aunt Amelia scolded. "And, Faried, you're soaked through! What have you two been up to?"

"Now, now," Uncle Faried interrupted her. "It was a very good thing for us that Armien was on board. But before either of us says anything more, I think that we could all do with a good breakfast. Especially our hero. Hey, Armien?"

Uncle Faried lifted Armien up onto his shoulders and carried him out of the harbor and up the road, with half of Kalk Bay still shouting and running behind them.

Aunt Amelia stared after them. "They've all gone mad," she decided finally. "But mad or not, they'll still need a hot breakfast." And she picked up her basket and hurried over to the cafe for two dozen fresh eggs, a string of sausages, and a loaf of good brown bread.